School Trouble
for
Andy
Russell

School Trouble
for
Andy Russell

David A. Adler

With illustrations by

Will Hillenbrand

SCHOLASTIC INC.
New York Toronto London Auckland Sydney
Mexico City New Delhi Hong Kong Buenos Aires

For my eldest son, Michael,
family role model,
leader, and sage

ISBN 0-439-32515-3

Text copyright © 1999 by David A. Adler.
Illustrations copyright © 1999 by Will Hillenbrand.
All rights reserved.
Published by Scholastic Inc., 555 Broadway, New York, NY 10012,
by arrangement with Harcourt, Inc.
SCHOLASTIC and associated logos are trademarks and/or
registered trademarks of Scholastic Inc.

12 11 10 9 8 7 6 5 4 3 2   2 3 4 5 6 7/0

Printed in the U.S.A.   40

First Scholastic printing, January 2002

Text set in Century Old Style
Designed by Kaelin Chappell

Contents

Contents

Chapter 1
The Round-Bodied,
Brown-Haired Jailer

Teachers in cages! Andy thought. *Now, that's a great idea! And principals and sisters, too!*

Andy pointed his pointing finger at his head and told himself, *Good work up there! Now tell me, why are they all in cages?*

Andy thought for a moment and then answered his own question. *They're in cages because they're in a zoo, a people zoo.*

Andy knew it was never too early to think about

1

his future, and right now he was sure he had found his vocation. He would become a zoo-keeper. *But in my zoo, people will be in cages and animals will roam free. I'll make money selling food to the animals to feed the people. I'll sell the animals cheeseburgers and fries and diet sodas. And I'll have signs posted.*

> PEOPLE HAVE SPECIAL DIETS
> PLEASE, DO NOT THROW
> FRUITS OR VEGETABLES
> INTO THE CAGES.
> *Zookeeper Andy Russell*

And Andy imagined the names he would give his caged people. Andy decided, *I'll call my teacher, Ms. Roman, a ROUND-BODIED, BROWN-HAIRED JAILER, and the principal, Mr. Harris, a GRISLY, FAT VESTED SCREAMER. I'll call my sister, Rachel, a TOO-NEAT PESTY DRUDGE.*

Andy smiled.

That's what I'll be, he decided, *the zookeeper of the first people zoo.*

Just then a large shadow darkened the area around Andy's desk.

Oh my, Andy thought, *it's getting dark! It's going to rain! I'll have to get my people into the covered parts of their cages.*

Then Andy remembered where he was. He looked up and saw his teacher, Ms. Roman, standing there.

"Andrew Russell, what are you doing here?" she asked.

"I'm learning," Andy answered. "That's why I'm in class."

"And is that where you belong?"

"Sure it is. I come here every day, except Saturdays, Sundays, and holidays," Andy said. "I come here to get an education."

Ms. Roman glared down at Andy.

What did I do now? Andy wondered.

"Look around the room," Ms. Roman told Andy, "and please explain to me why you're still here."

Andy looked. He and Ms. Roman were the only ones in the room.

"Oops!" Andy said.

" 'Oops!' is right," Ms. Roman replied. "The bell for lunch rang five minutes ago and you didn't even hear it. And if you didn't hear the lunch bell, I'm sure you didn't hear my math lesson."

Ms. Roman was right. Andy hadn't heard the math lesson. The last thing he'd heard was Ms. Roman teaching geography and talking about lakes and rivers.

"I'll pay attention this afternoon. I promise, I will," Andy said. Quickly, he closed his notebook before Ms. Roman could see it was open to the geography section.

Ms. Roman asked, "But what about the math lesson you missed?"

Andy knew that was one of those rhetorical questions—the kind you don't answer.

"Your mother's a high school math teacher," Ms. Roman said. "Perhaps this weekend she can teach you the math you missed. And to prove you know the work, you'll do all the problems at the end of chapter seven."

"Yes, Ms. Roman," Andy said, and reached in his desk for his lunch bag.

"I wonder," Ms. Roman said slowly as Andy stood up, "if you were listening when I taught chapters one through six."

"Sure I was," Andy said.

"Good. Then you will have no trouble doing all the problems at the ends of those chapters, too."

Ms. Roman smiled, then added, "It's Friday, so you have all weekend to do them. I expect them to be on my desk Monday morning."

"But I already did them," Andy protested. "I handed them in."

"And you'll do them again," Ms. Roman told him as she turned and walked to the front of the room.

I better get out of here fast, Andy thought, *before she thinks of some more work for me to do.*

Andy took his lunch and hurried to the lunchroom. He went to his regular place near the window, with his classmates Tamika Anderson, Bruce Jeffries, and Stacy Ann Jackson. He dropped his lunch bag on the table and said, "I thought you were my friends. How could you leave me there, alone with that ROUND-BODIED, BROWN-HAIRED JAILER?"

"With what?" Stacy Ann asked.

"With Ms. Roman," Andy explained. "Now I have to do seven chapters of math problems over the weekend."

"I'm sorry," Tamika replied. "We tried to wake you, but Ms. Roman wouldn't let us. She told us to leave the room quietly. She said she wanted to see how long it would take you to realize we had all gone to lunch."

"I wasn't sleeping," Andy said as he sat down. "I was thinking about my future. And I'm glad that by next year I'll have some other teacher and not Ms. Roman."

"You better get to work," Stacy Ann warned. "If you don't, next year you'll still be in fourth grade."

Andy shuddered. The very thought of another year with Ms. Roman made him lose his appetite. He pushed his lunch bag across the table and told Bruce, "You can have this."

"I can?" Bruce asked, and opened the bag. "Thanks. You know," he said as he unwrapped Andy's cream-cheese sandwich, "I tried to wake you. I made scary faces at you and waved my hands, but you just sat there."

Stacy Ann told Bruce, "You looked silly."

Bruce turned to Stacy Ann and said sweetly, "I hope I didn't scare you."

Stacy Ann twisted her head to the side, stuck out her tongue, blinked her eyes, and said, "This is what you did and it's not scary. It's just silly."

Bruce explained, "I was only trying to be a good friend to Andy."

Bruce bit into the sandwich. Then he waved his right hand frantically and pointed to Andy's lunch bag.

"Oh, stop trying to scare us," Stacy Ann told him.

Bruce shook his head and pointed again to the lunch bag.

"What do you want?" Tamika asked.

Bruce's mouth was full of white bread and cream cheese. He couldn't talk.

Tamika gave him the lunch bag. Bruce reached in, took out an apple, and bit into it. After he swallowed, he said, "That sandwich is dry."

"I'm sorry," Andy said sarcastically. "Next time I'll have my father use the *juicy* cream cheese."

Bruce alternated between biting the sandwich and the apple. Tamika and Stacy Ann talked about Ms. Roman. They thought she looked tired. And Andy thought about Ms. Roman. *Why does she hate me?* he wondered.

RRRR!

The bell rang. Lunch period was over.

Children hurried out of the lunchroom.

Tamika, Bruce, and Stacy Ann got up to leave, too.

"Wait!" Andy said. "I forgot to feed Cobalt."

8

Cobalt was a kitten Andy and Stacy Ann had found in the school playground.

"I fed her," Stacy Ann said. "I gave her a container of milk."

Andy and his friends quickly left the lunchroom.

"She'll be watching me," Andy said as they walked back to class.

"Cobalt?" Bruce asked.

"No," Andy replied. "Ms. Roman. She just loves getting me into trouble. But this afternoon I'll listen to every word she says, just like you do, Stacy Ann."

"Good luck," Stacy Ann Jackson said.

That afternoon Andy tried to pay attention in class, but every time he looked at Ms. Roman, he imagined her in a people-zoo cage with this sign in front:

WARNING. KEEP AWAY!
THIS ROUND-BODIED,
BROWN-HAIRED JAILER
IS VICIOUS!
Zookeeper Andy Russell

When the bell rang and the school day ended, Andy was in a hurry to get out of the classroom, but Ms. Roman stopped him.

She smiled and said, "During lunch period I called and spoke to your mother. She's anxious to help you with the math."

She's anxious to punish *me,* Andy thought as he ran to the bus. *That's what she's anxious to do.*

Andy sat in the back of the bus with Tamika and Bruce. They talked about what they would do over the weekend. But Andy just looked out the window. He knew what he would be doing. Math!

Chapter 2
Roman Holiday

The bus stopped across the street from Andy's house. He got off along with his sister, Rachel, Tamika, and the Belmont girls. Rachel was older than Andy, so she carried the house key. She went to middle school, in the building next to Andy's.

"Tonight Mom and Dad are taking us to that new bear movie," Rachel told Andy and Tamika as she unlocked the door. "I heard it's real scary."

Rachel and Tamika took their backpacks upstairs.

Tamika's parents had been in a car accident. While they were in a rehabilitation center, slowly recovering, Tamika had first lived next door with the Perlmans. When the Perlmans left to travel for their work, Tamika moved in with the Russells. Rachel was sharing her room with Tamika.

Andy dropped his backpack in the hall and went to the basement to check on his pet snake, gerbils, and goldfish.

Andy looked in his snake's tank first.

"Hi, Slither," Andy said.

Slither didn't turn to look at Andy.

Andy waved his hands. He stuck out his tongue, but still Slither didn't look.

"Hey, aren't you interested in looking at me?" Andy asked. "I look at you."

Slither didn't answer, so Andy looked at his gerbils. They were busy eating, drinking, and running on their exercise wheels and through their tunnels. None of them stopped to look at Andy.

"You'll look at me, won't you?" Andy asked his goldfish, Sylvia.

Sylvia swam to the front of the tank and did look

at Andy, but only for a moment. Then she swam away.

"Hey, what are you doing?" Tamika asked as she went down the basement steps.

"I'm getting bad news," Andy told her. "My animals are telling me I have to find a new career."

"A *new* career! What was your old one?"

"I was going to be a zookeeper," Andy said. "That's what I was thinking about when everyone in class went to lunch and left me with Ms. Roman. But my zoo was going to have people in cages, and animals would look at *us*."

"You're strange," Tamika said.

"But Sylvia is the only one who will look at me," Andy added. "And if I put the zoo underwater so goldfish can come, the cheeseburgers would get soggy, the diet-soda bubbles would float away, and the people would drown!"

"Huh?" Tamika asked.

Andy shook his head and told her, "I don't think my people-zoo idea will work. Too many problems."

"That's too bad," Tamika said as she sat on the couch. "I came down here to ask if you want me to help you with your other problems—

your math problems. I could do two or three chapters."

"Thanks," Andy said, "but I'll do it. It's my punishment, not yours."

When Andy's parents came home, Mrs. Russell told Andy, "Ms. Roman called and told me about all the math work you have. It's too bad you won't be able to go to the movie tonight."

"Sure I can, Mom. I'll do all that work tomorrow and Sunday."

"You don't understand," Mr. Russell explained. "Ms. Roman is punishing you, and so are we. Mom is taking the girls to the movie. I'm staying home with you."

All weekend Andy wasn't allowed to watch television or play his video games. And the math work took longer than he thought it would. He was almost glad when the weekend ended and he could go back to school.

"Here," Andy said when he went into class Monday morning and put his punishment assignment on Ms. Roman's desk. "Here are all the math problems."

Ms. Roman was sitting by her desk. She smiled at Andy.

Andy didn't smile back.

"Try to pay attention today," Ms. Roman told him. "I don't enjoy punishing you."

Sure you do, Andy thought. *That's why you're smiling.*

When class began, Ms. Roman said, "Read 'The Steadfast Tin Soldier' by Hans Christian Andersen. It begins on page seventy-three of your readers. Then write a summary of the story."

Ms. Roman sat at her desk and watched as Andy and the others read the story.

Maybe I'll become a teacher, like Ms. Roman, Andy thought. *I'll tell kids to do stuff and then watch them work.*

Then Andy realized, *If I become a teacher, I'll be in school until I'm an old man!*

He decided he'd have to find some other job.

Andy read "The Steadfast Tin Soldier" and then wrote, "It's about a tin soldier and what happened to it."

A summary should be short, Andy thought, *and mine is* real *short, so it's* real *good!*

He looked up at Ms. Roman. She was writing math problems on the board. "After you have finished reading and writing your summary, please copy and solve these division problems," Ms. Roman said. Then she sat at her desk, in front of the room.

More math! Andy thought. *More busywork, just like those seven chapters of problems. Hasn't anyone told her about calculators?*

Andy copied the problems. Then he picked numbers at random and wrote them as answers. *This isn't a test,* Andy reasoned. *And she's not even going to look at my answers. I can get these all wrong and it won't matter.*

When Andy was done, he thought about his future again. *Maybe I can become a great film director,* Andy thought. *I'll make animal movies.*

Then Andy thought about Slither. *I can use some of my toy cars and let Slither slither over them. Compared to those miniatures, Slither will look like a giant python. I'll take pictures, and if that works, I'll use the video camera next and make my own horror film.*

"Hey, Andy," Cory Davis whispered, "take a look at Ms. Roman. I think she's asleep."

Andy looked at Ms. Roman. Her arms were folded on her desk. Her head was resting on them and her eyes were closed.

"So what?" Andy whispered to Cory. "Sometimes I sleep in class, too."

"Watch this," Cory said. He frantically waved both his hands.

Ms. Roman didn't respond.

Cory got out of his seat and made strange faces at Ms. Roman, but her eyes remained closed.

Cory continued to make faces as he quietly tiptoed to the front of the room. Some children giggled, and Cory put his finger to his lips to quiet them.

Cory stood close to Ms. Roman. He watched her and waited. When he was sure she was asleep, he wrote on the chalkboard, NO HOMEWORK TONIGHT. NO SCHOOL TOMORROW. He thought for a moment and then added, IT'S A ROMAN HOLIDAY!

Stacy Ann Jackson sat at the desk just in front of Andy's. She turned and asked, "What's the matter with Ms. Roman?"

Andy shrugged. He didn't know. He'd rather think about Slither and becoming a great movie director.

I'll call my first movie, Giant Snake Eats New York. *It will be a hit,* Andy thought, *and when I'm a movie director, I'll have lots of helpers. They'll help*

me make the movies and they'll do division problems for me.

"Hey," Cory said as he returned to his seat. He said it in a loud whisper, loud enough for the other children to hear. "Let's all leave the room. When Ms. Roman wakes up, we'll all be gone."

"Like what you did to me on Friday?" Andy asked.

"Yeah," Cory answered. "That was funny."

Stacy Ann said, "Well, I'm not going."

"I can't go yet," Andy's friend Bruce said. "I didn't finish the division problems."

"Your teacher is sleeping!" Cory told Bruce. "You don't have to do any problems!" Then he looked at the others and complained, "What kind of a class is this? Ms. Roman is asleep! We should be having fun!"

Cory said that a little too loud. Ms. Roman looked up. Her skin was pale. Her eyes were red.

"Oops!" Cory said. He quickly sat in his seat and did the division problems.

Ms. Roman looked at the class. Everyone but Andy was still at work.

"Andrew Russell, are you done?" Ms. Roman asked.

Andy held up his notebook and said, "I have an answer to every problem."

"You see," Ms. Roman said slowly, "all the math work you did over the weekend helped you. I'll bet that now you're one of my top math students."

Andy smiled. He was glad she didn't take a close look at his answers. He was sure they were all wrong.

Ms. Roman sat at her desk, with her red eyes open until the bell rang and it was time for lunch.

Ms. Roman waved weakly. "You may go," she said. Then she rested her head on her arms again and closed her eyes.

In the lunchroom, Andy sat with Tamika, Stacy Ann, and Bruce.

Stacy Ann asked, "Did you see Ms. Roman? She looks terrible. I think she's sick."

"Do we have to talk about her?" Andy asked. "Let's talk about my new career. I'm going to be a movie director."

"You are?" Bruce asked. "And guess what?"

No one guessed.

"Come on," Bruce said.

"The stuffed animals on your bed spoke to you last night," Andy suggested. "They told you to move over."

"No, really. I'm serious," Bruce said. Then he turned to Stacy Ann and said, "And I don't sleep with stuffed animals anymore."

"Bruce," Andy said slowly, "why don't you just tell us?"

"You're going to be a movie director," Bruce said, "and I'm going to be an actor."

Bruce reached out and took Stacy Ann's hand. He looked at her and said softly, "Your eyes are deep, blue pools." He touched his heart and added, "And I wish to swim in them."

Stacy Ann pulled her hand away and said, "Yuck! Who wants you swimming in my eyeballs?"

"That was acting," Bruce told her.

"That was disgusting," Stacy Ann said.

"Ms. Roman's eyes are deep, *red* pools," Tamika said. "I'm worried about her. I think she's sick."

Andy looked at his watch. "Hey, we have to hurry and eat."

They ate quickly and then fed Cobalt. When

lunchtime ended and they returned to class, a thin young woman with curly blond hair and dark blue pants was standing at the front of the room. She was holding a pile of papers.

"I am Ms. Salmon," she said very slowly as she walked from desk to desk and handed each child a math work sheet. "Unfortunately, Ms. Roman is indisposed. For the remainder of the school day, I will be your teacher."

Great! Andy thought. *With Ms. Roman gone, I won't get into any trouble.*

"A substitute!" Cory whispered. "Watch this!"

When Ms. Salmon handed Cory a work sheet, he let it drop. Just as Ms. Salmon bent to pick it up, Cory tore a sheet of paper. It sounded like cloth ripping.

"I see London," Cory said real loud, "I see France. I see Salmon's underpants."

"Oh my!" she cried.

Children laughed.

Ms. Salmon dropped the work sheets, held her hands behind her, and ran from the room.

"Now," Cory told his classmates, "everybody, turn your desks and chairs around. When fishy

Ms. Salmon comes back, she'll be all mixed-up."

"Yeah," one of the boys in front said.

"Great idea," someone added.

Andy watched Cory and many others in the class turn their desks and chairs to face the chalkboard in the back of the room. Then Andy did, too.

"I'm not doing it," Stacy Ann said. "It's silly."

It is *silly,* Andy thought, *but so what! I'd rather be silly than have to spend the afternoon with Ms. Roman.*

Andy looked at the work sheet—forty multiplication problems. *More math!* he thought. *Here I go again.*

Andy chose numbers at random and wrote them as answers. He was almost done when the door opened and the principal, Mr. Harris, walked in, followed by Ms. Salmon. They walked to the back of the room and faced the class.

There he is, Andy thought, *the* GRISLY, FAT VESTED SCREAMER.

Ms. Salmon pointed to Cory Davis and whispered, "That's him."

"What you did wasn't funny," Mr. Harris told

Cory. Then he looked across the room and asked, "Stacy Ann Jackson, why are you facing the wrong way?"

Stacy Ann slowly turned her desk and chair around. She looked up at Mr. Harris and said, "I was facing the right way. *Now* I'm the wrong way."

Mr. Harris didn't seem to hear Stacy Ann. He stood for a long while and looked intently at each child, one at a time.

Andy didn't want to be stared at. It made him uncomfortable. So he looked down at his work sheet.

Then Mr. Harris looked directly at Cory.

"I don't want Ms. Salmon to complain about you again," he said. Then he looked across the room and added, "I expect each of you to be-have."

Andy's desk was in the back of the room, but now, with all of them turned around, it seemed it was in the front; and Mr. Harris was standing right there. He looked at Andy's work sheet and said to the class, "At least one student is doing his work."

Mr. Harris took Andy's paper and looked at it.

"What's this?" he asked Andy. "Fifty-three multiplied by nineteen is thirty-eight? That's not right. It's not even close!"

Mr. Harris looked at the work sheet again.

"None of these are right!" he said. "It looks to me like you just guessed. Erase these answers and do the work as carefully as you would for Ms. Roman."

That's what I did! Andy thought.

Mr. Harris waited for everyone to get to work.

"Remember," Mr. Harris announced, "this is not playtime!" Then he left the room.

Andy looked at the work sheet. Forty multiplication problems! He turned and looked at his classmates, who were now sitting behind him. They were busy multiplying.

Andy looked at Cory. He was multiplying, too.

Andy blamed Cory for his latest trouble. *If the desks were facing the right way, Mr. Harris would not have seen my work!*

"*This is not playtime!*" Andy thought as he looked at his paper. *It sure isn't!*

$$53$$
$$\times\ 19$$

Nine times three equals twenty-seven, Andy said to himself. He wrote a seven beneath the nine and a two above the five.

I shouldn't be doing this now! Andy thought. *I should be planning my movie.*

But Andy did the problems, anyway, one after another until the bell rang.

Chapter 3
Andy Loves Animals

Please pass your papers to the front of the room," Ms. Salmon said.

Everybody in Andy's row passed their papers to him. "Hey," Andy complained. "Why are you giving them to me?" Then he realized that now *he* was at the front of the room.

Andy gave the work sheets from his row to Ms. Salmon.

"Thank you for your cooperation," Ms. Salmon told the class. "You are now officially dismissed."

"Great, I'm officially dismissed," Andy mumbled as he packed his backpack. "And now Mr. Harris knows I guess at my math problems. I'm officially in trouble again."

Andy hurried to catch up with Tamika and Bruce to get on his bus.

"Hey, Andy!" Cory called to him in the hall. "Didn't we have fun with fishy Ms. Salmon?"

"Maybe you had fun," Andy said as they walked though the hall, "but because of you, I got in trouble."

"Because of me? I didn't write those not-even-close answers on your paper. You did. And anyway, I got in trouble, too."

Andy stopped and faced Cory.

"Mr. Harris wouldn't have seen my paper if we hadn't turned our desks around. I would have been in the back of the room, where I belong. That's why I sit there, because I don't want to be bothered by teachers and principals."

Cory asked, "Is it my fault you got all the answers wrong?"

"Well, it's your fault Mr. Harris came into the room," Andy answered. "All a substitute wants is for us to be quiet. And I *was* quiet. But because of you, I had to do math problems. I'm *sick* of math problems!"

"Admit it," Cory said. "It was funny when she thought her pants tore."

Andy smiled and agreed, "Yeah, it was funny, but it was the beginning of trouble for me."

Andy looked around. Children were hurrying out of the school. He didn't see Tamika and Bruce.

"Hey!" Andy said, and started to run off. "Now because of you, I'm going to miss the bus."

Andy ran past a group of children who were coming out of the art room.

"Watch out!" he called to two kindergarten girls who were holding hands.

They quickly let go of each other's hands, and Andy ran between the girls.

"No running in the halls!" Mr. Harris shouted.

Andy slowed down and said, "But I'm going to miss my bus."

Buses were lined up outside of Andy's school and the middle school. The doors of most of the buses were closed. The motors of the ones at the beginning of the line were running. Andy's bus was first in line and was already leaving.

"Hey, wait for me!" Andy shouted, and ran past

the line of buses. He waved his arms. "Wait for me!"

Andy's bus kept moving. The one behind it started going, too.

A crossing guard was standing at the end of the circular drive. He had his left hand held up to stop cars on the street in front of the school. With his right hand he was waving for the buses to go.

"Stop the bus! Stop the bus!" Andy shouted, but with all the noise—the buses' motors running and the children talking and shouting—no one heard Andy.

The third and then the fourth bus in line rolled past.

Andy stopped running.

More trouble! Andy thought. *Now I have to call Mom at her school and ask her to pick me up. She hates that. I wish I lived closer to school and I could walk home.*

Just then the crossing guard held up his right hand, signaling the buses to stop. Andy walked quickly toward his bus. When he got close, he saw a cat and four kittens. The crossing guard had stopped the buses so the cat family could safely cross the street.

"Thank you," Andy said to the cat and her kittens. Then he knocked on the door of his bus. It opened.

"I'm sorry," Mr. Cole, the driver, said as Andy stepped in. "Tamika and Bruce asked me to wait, but I couldn't. I was the first in line today. I just couldn't keep all the other buses waiting."

"That's OK," Andy said.

Andy turned and watched the last of the kittens climb onto the sidewalk, and told Mr. Cole, "I love animals."

"I love them, too," Mr. Cole said. "Now hurry and find a seat."

Chapter 4
I Am an Actor

"Hi, monkey face," Rachel said to Andy as he walked down the aisle between the seats on the bus.

"Yeah, sure," Andy replied.

"Back here!" Bruce called, and waved. "I saved you a seat."

Bruce was sitting next to Tamika on the long seat in the back of the bus. Andy quickly joined them.

"Did you see that?" Andy asked. "You couldn't

get Mr. Cole to wait, but a cat and four kittens did. I love animals."

Tamika was sitting by the window. She watched the cat and kittens walk along the sidewalk and said, "They're cute."

" 'This is not playtime!' " Andy said, mimicking Mr. Harris. "Of course it's not playtime. Who ever has fun in school?"

"I'll bet those kittens are just a few weeks old," Tamika said.

"Do you think they need a place to live?" Andy asked.

"Don't even think about bringing them home," Tamika told him. "Your family is still adjusting to having me in the house."

"You're easy," Andy said. "I heard my parents say you're helpful and polite. They also said they hoped I would learn from you." Andy shook his head and added, "You're not the one they're adjusting to. It's me!"

"Well," Tamika said, "Rachel is adjusting to me. She told me that last night I moved in my sleep, knocked into the wall, and woke her up."

Andy told Tamika, "Rachel always complains."

"And she said that before I moved in, she laid

out her clothes for the next day on the extra bed and now I'm in it."

"Tell her it's for her own good," Andy said. "Rachel should wait until morning to choose her clothes. Otherwise, there might be a yellow shirt on the bed when she's in a purple-shirt mood."

Tamika shook her head and said, "I don't think Rachel has purple-shirt moods."

Andy, Tamika, and Bruce sat quietly for a while. Then Andy told them his plans for a movie starring Slither.

"And since I'm going to be an actor, I'll be in it. Right?" Bruce asked.

Andy nodded.

Bruce thought for a moment and then said, "Listen to this!"

He stood, spread out his arms dramatically, and said real loud, "No! Stop! Get away, you snake—you viper, you killer!"

Children on the bus turned to see what was happening.

Bruce held his hands up, clenched his fists, and said even louder, "So, you won't get away! Now you'll be sorry! You'll feel the power of Bruce!"

"STOP THAT!" Mr. Cole shouted. "STOP FIGHTING!"

"I'm not fighting," Bruce said, "I'm acting."

"THEN STOP ACTING AND SIT DOWN!" Mr. Cole shouted.

"Wasn't I great?" Bruce asked Andy, as he sat down. "Mr. Cole really thought I was being attacked by a snake. I told you. I'm a great actor."

"Sure," Andy said sarcastically. "And a great fighter, too, with the 'power of Bruce.'"

The bus had stopped.

"Hey, Bruce!" Mr. Cole called out. "Don't you live here? Shouldn't you be getting off now?"

"Yeah," Rachel called from the front of the bus, "why don't you act like a tree and leave?"

"I can do that," Bruce said. He got up and bowed dramatically to Andy and Tamika. He turned and bowed to the other children and then to Mr. Cole.

Andy applauded. Many children joined him as Bruce hurried down the aisle and off the bus.

Andy, Tamika, Rachel, and the two Belmont girls got off at the next stop.

"What's with Bruce?" the short Belmont girl asked Andy.

Andy told her, "He was just having fun."

"Screaming on a bus isn't fun," the tall Belmont girl said. "It's rude."

"And what's wrong with Ms. Roman?" Rachel asked as they crossed the street. "First I saw her sitting in the nurse's office. Then I saw Mr. Harris helping her into a taxicab."

"She's sick," Andy said. "She even fell asleep in class."

"She's probably sick of you," Rachel told her brother.

"Yeah," Andy admitted. "She probably is." He was about to add, "And I'm sick of Ms. Roman." But he didn't.

"She was really pale," Tamika said, "and her eyes were red."

Rachel unlocked the front door of the Russells' house and opened it. Against the wall, just inside the door, was Mrs. Russell's book bag.

"Mom is home," Rachel said. "I'm going up to see her."

As Rachel went upstairs, Andy whispered to Tamika, "Mom usually does shopping after work, but Mr. Harris probably called her at school and told her about that work sheet. That's why she came home early, to punish me again."

Andy watched Rachel walk toward their parents' room. He waited, then he said, "It's no use putting it off. I may as well go up there and be yelled at."

"Good luck," Tamika said.

Andy waited until Rachel came out of his parents' room. Then he slowly walked up the stairs and entered his parents' bedroom. Mrs. Russell was lying on the bed. Her eyes were closed.

"It's not my fault," Andy said. "Well, it really is, but why did I have to do all those problems, anyway? It was just to keep us quiet, and I *was* quiet."

Mrs. Russell opened her eyes and asked, "Andy, what are you talking about?"

It was obvious to Andy that Mr. Harris hadn't called, so he quickly changed the subject.

"Hey, Mom, why are you in bed?" he asked. "Are you sick?"

"I'm not sick. I'm just tired," Mrs. Russell replied. "I had a hard day, and sometimes doing all the shopping and helping take care of the house and being pregnant are just too much for me."

"If I were you, Mom, I'd have that baby already."

Mrs. Russell laughed. She put her hands on her stomach and said, "He's not ready yet. There are some things that just can't be rushed."

Mrs. Russell sat up, smiled, and said, "You know, Andy, when I was pregnant with you, it seemed you were never coming out. You were having too much fun in here kicking."

"I know," Andy said. "You already told me I kicked a lot."

"You kicked so much," Mrs. Russell said, "I thought you'd be born wearing cleats and a football uniform."

"Imagine that," Andy said, "a football player with a smelly diaper. They could burp me in the huddles."

Mrs. Russell smiled and said, "Now, tell me what happened in school. Did you get in trouble with Ms. Roman again?"

"No. It was with Mr. Harris. We had a substitute this afternoon, and she gave us a math worksheet, and I didn't do the problems. I guessed at the answers."

"You know math is important," Mrs. Russell said.

"I know," Andy admitted, "but I'm tired of it."

Andy changed the subject again.

"Ms. Roman went home sick," he told his mother.

"Oh my," Mrs. Russell said. "I hope this time it's not serious."

"'This time'?" Andy asked.

"Well," Mrs. Russell said slowly, "Ms. Roman was sick a few years ago. She was absent from school for almost two months."

"Two months!" Andy said.

Two months without Ms. Roman, Andy thought. *Maybe this wasn't such a bad day.*

Chapter 5
Protein Surprise

Mrs. Russell got up off the bed and said to Andy, "I have tests to grade and I'm sure you have homework to do."

Andy followed his mother downstairs. Mrs. Russell emptied her book bag onto the dining-room table and worked there. Andy sat with Tamika in the kitchen.

As Andy took his books out of his backpack, he told Tamika, "This is a waste of time. We're doing homework, and Ms. Roman probably won't be in school tomorrow. She may not be in school for two months."

He told her what his mother had said about the last time Ms. Roman was sick.

"Well," Tamika said as she opened her geography book, "this homework is interesting. And anyway, if I don't do it, I have to hope Ms. Roman will be absent and I don't really want that. I like her."

"Well, I don't," Andy said. "She makes me work too hard. I wish she just left me alone. Why does she care if I know how to divide and how long the Mississippi River is? Why does anyone care?"

Tamika didn't respond. She knew Andy was still upset about the punishment math assignment.

Andy reluctantly opened his notebook and did the homework, too. He did the math and geography on his own. Then he compared his answers with Tamika's to be sure his answers were right.

They had finished their work and were talking about the Slither movie Andy would make, when Mr. Russell came home. He asked them to talk somewhere else. "I don't want anyone to watch me while I prepare dinner," Mr. Russell said.

"Do you have a new secret recipe?" Andy asked.

Mr. Russell smiled and said, "I'm not telling."

Tamika closed her books, put them in her backpack, and said, "We're done."

"Yeah," Andy replied. "We're done. We'll go downstairs and you can make potfuls of potions."

"I'm not making potions," Mr. Russell told Andy. "I'm just making dinner, and I want to do it alone."

"OK," Andy said, and left the kitchen with Tamika.

Andy first visited his gerbils. "Hi, guys," he said, and checked that their water bottles were full and there was food in their bowls.

"Hi, Sylvia," he said to the goldfish, and sprinkled in a few flakes of food. He watched her swim to the top of the tank to eat.

Then Andy checked the snake tank. Slither ate minnows. There were two swimming in a small bowl at the bottom of his tank.

Slither stuck out his forked tongue.

"You should be nice to me," Andy advised the snake. "I'm the one who keeps your bowl filled with minnows, and I'm the one who's going to make you a movie star."

Slither answered by sticking his forked tongue out again. Andy responded by sticking *his* spoon-shaped tongue out at Slither.

"Are you two ready to get to work?" Tamika asked.

Slither didn't answer, but Andy did. He said he was ready. Andy put a large sheet of white cardboard on the floor. He and Tamika drew roads and houses on it. Then they arranged miniature cars along the roads.

"Wait here," Andy told Tamika. "I'll get the camera."

Andy went upstairs. As soon as he entered the kitchen, Mr. Russell threw a dish towel over a large aluminum pan.

"May I use your camera?" Andy asked.

"Yes, it's in my closet, on the shelf," Mr. Russell said. "I think there's film in it."

Andy went to his parents' room for the camera. On his way downstairs he stopped and looked in the kitchen. The dish towel was still covering the pan.

"You'll just have to wait," Mr. Russell told Andy.

Andy stood at the entrance to the kitchen and said, "Well, I'm waiting."

Mr. Russell shook his head. "No. You'll have to wait until dinner."

Andy shrugged and went downstairs, to the basement. He told Tamika, "Dad is doing something spooky with food, and he expects us to eat it."

Tamika said, "I'm sure it will be very good."

"You can eat it," Andy said. "But I'm not. If I don't know what goes in the food, the food doesn't go in me."

Tamika laughed.

"What's so funny?" Andy asked.

"That's such a great quote," she answered. "Like 'Give me liberty or give me death!' "

"And 'Don't fire until you see the whites of their eggs,' " Andy said.

"Eyes!" Tamika corrected. "William Prescott said, 'Don't fire until you see the whites of their eyes,' not 'eggs'! He said it during the Revolutionary War and he meant wait until the enemy is real close before you shoot."

"Eyes, eggs—whatever," Andy said, and gave Tamika the camera. There were four pictures left on the roll of film.

Andy went to Slither's tank. "First, Tamika will

take still pictures of you," he said as he slid off the screen on the top of the tank, "and if they look good, I'll put you in a movie."

Andy took Slither from the tank and put him on the cardboard. "Be nice to me," Andy told Slither, "and I'll make you a star."

Slither slithered and pushed aside the toy cars.

Click. A bright flash lit up the basement.

Andy held Slither and rearranged the cars. "Now, pretend you're a python," Andy instructed the snake. "Act vicious."

Andy put Slither on the cardboard again.

Slither curled his bottom half into a tight coil, stretched out his top, and stuck out his forked tongue.

Click.

"Great!" Andy declared. "That's acting!"

Click.

Tamika informed Andy that just one picture remained on the roll of film.

"This is it," Andy told Slither. "You have to make this one good."

Andy took the miniature sports car and tried to put it in Slither's mouth, but the toy fell out.

Tamika was still looking at Slither through the

camera's viewfinder. "Maybe he doesn't like sports cars," she said.

Andy tried a toy Jeep and a motorcycle, but they both fell out.

Tamika put the camera down and said, "This isn't working."

"Keep looking through the camera," Andy instructed. "I don't want you to miss a good picture."

Andy placed a handful of toy cars around Slither.

Slither hissed.

He stuck out his forked tongue.

Click.

The camera buzzed as it automatically rewound the film.

"That's it," Tamika told Andy. She opened the back of the camera, took out the film, and gave it to Andy. As Andy took the film, Slither slithered off the cardboard and onto the rug.

"How do you think these pictures will come out?" Andy asked.

Tamika shrugged and said, "Oh, the pictures will come out. But the cars may not look real."

Slither was under the table.

Tamika gathered the toys and put them away.

She looked in the snake tank. Then she looked at the floor. "Hey, where's Slither?" Tamika asked.

"Oh no!" Andy said. "Not again! I'm already in enough trouble."

Slither had gotten loose before, soon after Mr. Russell gave him to Andy as a reward for not getting in trouble for the last six weeks of third grade. And Andy's gerbils had gotten loose twice, too, once at home, before Tamika came to live with the Russells, and once in school, when some were given away as prizes at the fourth-grade carnival.

Andy and Tamika crawled on the floor and searched for Slither.

The basement door opened.

"Come upstairs," Mr. Russell said. "It's time for dinner."

"In a minute, Dad," Andy answered.

"There he is!" Tamika said.

"There's who?" Mr. Russell asked.

Tamika lunged toward the basement heater.

"I missed," she said.

"What's going on?" Mr. Russell asked as he walked down the stairs. "Are the gerbils or your snake loose again?"

Andy put both his hands under the heater, one on each side of Slither, and grabbed him.

"No," Andy said as he triumphantly held up Slither.

"Just for that," Andy told the snake as he put him in his tank, "your name will be *real* small on the movie posters and billboards."

Mr. Russell told Andy, "Make sure the screen of Slither's tank is completely closed."

Andy did. And he gave his father the roll of film. Then he, Tamika, and Mr. Russell went upstairs.

Mr. Russell put on two oven mitts. Mrs. Russell and Rachel were sitting at the kitchen table. Mrs. Russell said, "Now we're all here and I'm hungry. What's for dinner?"

"A dish towel," Andy said. "That's what's for dinner. Dad put it in a pan and cooked it." He sat down. "Hey, Dad, I want my towel well-done."

"It's not a dish towel," Mr. Russell said. "It's a surprise."

Mr. Russell opened the oven door. He took out an aluminum pan and put it on the tile trivet in the middle of the table.

"Hey, Dad, baked potatoes, tomatoes, and peppers are not much of a surprise," Rachel said.

The potatoes, tomatoes, and peppers were arranged in the pan in two neat rows. The top of each was cut but still in place, like a little hat. A few of the peppers had little paper umbrellas stuck in them.

"And not much of a dinner," Mrs. Russell said. "Where's the protein?"

"Don't be so quick to judge," Mr. Russell admonished.

Rachel took a baked tomato. She took off the tomato cap and said, "There's tuna inside."

"That's protein," Mr. Russell announced.

"And there's cheese in my potato," both Mrs. Russell and Tamika said.

"That's protein, too," Mr. Russell said.

Mrs. Russell ate some potato and cheese, and said, "Dinner is delicious."

"And a nice surprise," Tamika added.

Rachel held up her fork and saluted her father. "Bravo," she said.

Andy looked suspiciously at the baked pepper on his plate. He poked his fork at the pepper cap, and it fell onto his plate.

"Yuck!" he cried out. "Sardines! Slither eats little slimy fish. People don't!"

"Sardines are protein," Mr. Russell told Andy, "and I *do* eat them." He took the stuffed pepper from Andy's plate and put it on his own.

Andy took a tomato. "And I eat tuna," Andy informed his father. "It's a big fish."

Chapter 6
Big Trouble

The next morning, when Andy went into his classroom, Mr. Harris and Ms. Salmon were standing there. Andy quickly put his backpack beneath his chair. He sat, folded his hands on his desk, and waited. Mr. Harris and Ms. Salmon waited, too.

"Hurry up," Mr. Harris instructed the children standing near the coat closet and those just coming into the room. "Get into your seats and get ready to learn."

The desks were facing the front of the room again. Andy slid down in his seat and hid behind Stacy Ann Jackson. He was sitting in the back again, where he felt he belonged.

"Ms. Roman will be absent for a few days," Mr. Harris announced as he walked down the aisle toward Andy, "and Ms. Salmon will be your teacher."

When Mr. Harris reached Andy's desk, he stopped and said, "Sit up!"

Andy sat up.

Mr. Harris turned and walked toward the front of the room. "I expect everyone to pay attention and do his or her work," he said. He quickly turned, looked at Andy, and asked, "Is that clear, Andrew Russell?"

"Yes, Mr. Harris," Andy answered.

"And at the end of the day, I expect Ms. Salmon to tell me how well behaved you were." He walked to Cory's desk, stared down, and asked, "Is that clear, Cory Davis?"

"Yes, Mr. Harris," Cory answered softly. "That's clear."

"Now, open your notebooks," Mr. Harris said.

Everyone opened a notebook.

"Thank you," Ms. Salmon said to Mr. Harris. She folded her hands, looked up over the children's heads, and said slowly, "This morning you will hear a lecture on geography. Please turn to the proper section in your notebook."

When the school year began, Andy had divided his notebook into sections. But he had made some sections too small and some too big. Now whenever he had to write in his notebook, he just looked for an empty page.

"Have a good day," Mr. Harris said to Ms. Salmon, and left the room.

"Pencils in hand," Ms. Salmon instructed. "I expect you to take notes."

She waited. When she was sure each child was ready to write, she stood by the map hanging on the wall beside the chalkboard and began: "The Mississippi River flows from Minnesota to the Gulf of Mexico. It forms borders between many states."

"Hey, Andy," Cory whispered, "look what I got." Andy looked straight ahead.

Ms. Salmon pointed to the Mississippi River on the map and said, "It forms borders of Minnesota,

Iowa, Missouri, Arkansas, Louisiana, Wisconsin, Illinois, Tennessee, and Mississippi."

"Hey, Andy," Cory whispered again, "look over here."

Andy didn't look at Cory. Instead he wrote in his notebook, *The Mississippi River is very long.*

"Look here," Cory hissed.

Andy wrote, *It's the squiggly line between some states.*

"Hey, Andy," Cory hissed again, "I have a picture of you killing a snake."

Andy and Stacy Ann turned.

Andy looked at Cory and said in a loud, angry whisper, "No, you don't!"

Cory said, "Of course, I don't. But look what I *do* have."

Cory showed Andy and Stacy Ann fake vomit and rubber dog-excrement, a strip of Velcro, and an alarm clock.

Stacy Ann said, "That vomit and dog poop are disgusting!"

"What will you do with the Velcro and clock?" Andy asked.

"You'll see," Cory answered.

"You'll get into trouble," Stacy Ann warned.

And I won't *get into trouble,* Andy told himself. He turned to face Ms. Salmon. *I'm going to listen to all this river-border stuff, and even take notes.*

"The Missouri River is the longest river in the United States. It is formed in southwestern Montana," Ms. Salmon said. "It forms borders of South Dakota, Nebraska, Kansas, Iowa, and Missouri."

The Missouri River is wet, Andy wrote in his notebook. *It's very wet.*

Snap!

"Oh, my pencil broke!" Cory called out, and held up a pencil with a broken point.

He went to the front of the room, to the pencil sharpener behind the teacher's desk. While he sharpened his pencil, he watched Ms. Salmon. When she went to the map, Cory dropped a paper on her chair, and something else beside her desk. On his way back to his seat, Cory dropped something by the door to the room. Then he stopped by the coat closet, took something from his pocket, and placed it on the top shelf.

"The Ohio River," Ms. Salmon said slowly, "is in the eastern central section of the United States. It begins in Pittsburgh, Pennsylvania, and forms borders of Ohio, Illinois, Indiana, West Virginia, and Kentucky."

Ohio, Andy wrote in his notebook. He put a large dot inside both *O*s of Ohio and eyebrows on top. Then he extended the bottoms of the *h* and the *i* to form a large nose. Beneath the nose, he drew a mouth. He drew a large circle around it all, added ears and hair, and labeled his drawing SMILING OHIO.

Ms. Salmon spoke about the Rio Grande and the Colorado and Arkansas Rivers. While she spoke, Andy drew three more smiling Ohios. For one he used the side of his pencil point and shaded in lots of long hair, a beard, and a mustache.

"Now," Ms. Salmon said as she sat in the seat at her desk, "please open your geography textbooks to page one hundred and eighteen, chapter seven, 'Rivers of the United States.' Read to page one hundred and thirty-six and then answer all the questions at the end of the chapter."

Andy opened his geography text.

"The fun starts soon," Cory whispered, "real soon."

Look at this, Andy thought as he started to read:

"The end of a river is its mouth, where the water flows into a lake or an ocean or another river."

I'm so smart, Andy thought. *The Ohio River has a mouth, and so do my smiling Ohios.*

Andy read a few more paragraphs. Then he looked at the questions at the end of the chapter. He turned to a clean page in his notebook.

Andy looked at his pencil point. It was almost gone. *I used it up drawing hair on my smiling Ohios,* he thought.

Andy went to sharpen his pencil. Ms. Salmon got up so Andy could get by her.

Andy put his pencil in the sharpener and turned the handle.

"Hey, look!" Cory called out. He laughed and pointed at Ms. Salmon.

"What are you doing behind my back?" Ms. Salmon asked Andy. "Are you making silly faces?"

"No, Ms. Salmon," Andy answered. "I'm sharpening my pencil."

As Ms. Salmon turned to face Andy, other children laughed. Soon just about every child in the class was laughing and pointing at Ms. Salmon.

"Stop that!" Ms. Salmon shouted. She turned again to face the class. "Stop that!"

When Ms. Salmon turned, Andy saw why his classmates were laughing. Stuck to the seat of her pants was a sign: THIS IS SALMON'S FISH TAIL.

She turned to Andy and told him, "Stop making them laugh. Stop it!"

But the children kept laughing.

"You're in trouble," Ms. Salmon told Andy. "You're in BIG trouble now."

"What for?" Andy asked. "I didn't do anything except listen to you talk about rivers and Pittsburgh. I even took notes!"

The children were still laughing.

Ms. Salmon stepped forward and shouted, "Stop it! Stop laughing this instant!"

But they didn't stop.

Then Ms. Salmon looked down. "Oh my goodness, what did I step in?" she asked.

Andy looked down, too. Ms. Salmon had stepped in Cory's fake vomit.

Ms. Salmon poked it with the tip of her shoe. Then she picked it up and held it in front of Andy.

"More tricks!" she shouted at him. "You think this is funny?"

Andy's classmates did. Cory laughed so hard, he fell out of his chair.

RRRR!

A bell rang.

"The rest of you go to lunch," Ms. Salmon said. "I'm taking this young man to Mr. Harris."

"No!" Stacy Ann Jackson called out. "It's only ten o'clock. It's too early for lunch."

Daisy Barry sat near the coat closet. She took an alarm clock off the top shelf and told Ms. Salmon, "It was this."

"You've been a busy young man, haven't you?" Ms. Salmon asked Andy. "Well, now you'll have to keep busy somewhere else."

"ME?!" Andy shouted. "It wasn't me!"

But Ms. Salmon was sure Andy had caused all the trouble. "Come with me," she told him. "I'm taking you to Mr. Harris's office."

Chapter 7

Prisoner in the Principal's Office

"**B**ut I didn't do anything," Andy protested.

Ms. Salmon showed Andy the plastic vomit and the alarm clock, and asked him, "You call this nothing? Well, I don't! You just come with me."

Andy looked at Cory Davis.

Cory was not laughing now. He quickly looked down at his geography text and pretended to read.

Andy turned to Ms. Salmon and said again, "But I *didn't* do anything!"

"Are you telling me you don't know anything about this?" Ms. Salmon asked, and held up the fake vomit. "This imitation disgorge?"

"I didn't say I didn't know about it," Andy answered. "I said I didn't do it. I didn't put it on the floor. And I didn't put the clock in the closet. All I did was my work."

"And you made faces behind my back!" Ms. Salmon declared. "That's what you did! That's why everyone was laughing. You're coming with me."

Stacy Ann Jackson called out, "But Andy is telling the truth!"

Ms. Salmon turned. "It's you again!" she said, and pointed at Stacy Ann. "So, you're in this with him!"

"No, I'm not. We're just friends."

"Yesterday you turned your desk around," Ms. Salmon reminded Stacy Ann, "and embarrassed me in front of Mr. Harris, and now this!" Ms. Salmon waved the fake vomit. "This treachery!"

Stacy Ann looked at Cory.

His lips moved silently. He made signals with his hands, first to Stacy Ann and then to Andy, but neither Stacy Ann nor Andy understood what he was telling them.

"Tell her!" Stacy Ann said to Cory.

Cory shook his head and made more hand signals.

"Let's go," Ms. Salmon told Andy and Stacy Ann.

Stacy Ann looked again at Cory, but his head was down. He was pretending to read again.

"Tell her what?" Tamika asked Cory.

Cory didn't answer.

Andy and Stacy Ann followed Ms. Salmon to the door.

Suddenly Ms. Salmon stopped.

"What's this?" she asked as she took something brown off the floor. "Toy dog-droppings!"

She held them in front of Andy's face and asked, "Is this another joke of yours?"

Some children laughed.

"Well, I don't think it's funny," Ms. Salmon shouted, and the children stopped laughing. "Let's go!" she screamed at Andy and Stacy Ann. "We'll see what Mr. Harris thinks."

Ms. Salmon walked quickly out of the room. It was difficult for Andy and Stacy Ann to keep up with her. Andy pointed to the seat of Ms. Salmon's pants. The THIS IS SALMON'S FISH TAIL sign was still stuck there.

When Ms. Salmon was too far ahead to hear, Andy whispered to Stacy Ann, "What was Cory saying?"

"I don't know," Stacy Ann answered. "But don't worry. I'll tell Mr. Harris that someone else did all that stuff, but we can't say who it is. He knows I never get into trouble, so he'll believe me. He'll understand."

Andy shook his head and said, "I don't think so. I think somehow I'll get into even more trouble."

Ms. Salmon walked into the main office and past Mrs. Clark, the principal's secretary.

Andy and Stacy Ann followed her.

"Wait!" Mrs. Clark said. She quickly reached out and pulled the sign off Ms. Salmon's pants.

Ms. Salmon grabbed the sign, looked at it, and hissed, "Another prank!"

Ms. Salmon stormed into Mr. Harris's office. She slammed the sign, alarm clock, fake vomit, and dog excrement onto Mr. Harris's desk and screamed, "Do you see this? Do you see what these children, these ruffians, have done to me?"

The rubber droppings bounced across the desk. Mr. Harris had been writing. Now there was dog poop on his papers.

"They've ridiculed me," Ms. Salmon told Mr. Harris. "They've made it impossible for me to teach!"

Mr. Harris looked at the items on his desk. He looked at Andy and Stacy Ann, then at Ms. Salmon, and said softly, "You can go back to your room. I'll take care of this."

Ms. Salmon held up her right hand. She pointed at Andy and Stacy Ann. "These delinquents," she said, and waved her pointing finger, "these two have made me a joke to my students."

Mr. Harris nodded.

"They *must* be disciplined," Ms. Salmon said, and waved her pointing finger some more.

"I'll take care of this," Mr. Harris said again.

Ms. Salmon was shaking now. She jammed her hand into her pocket. She took a deep breath and thanked Mr. Harris. Then she left his office.

Mr. Harris went to his closet. He took out a

large envelope and wrote on it with a red marker, ANDREW RUSSELL AND STACY ANN JACKSON. He put the sign, clock, fake vomit, and excrement into the envelope.

"That's not our stuff," Stacy Ann told Mr. Harris.

Mr. Harris sat down behind his desk. He looked at Stacy Ann, but he didn't respond.

"Someone else put that sign on Ms. Salmon's pants," Stacy Ann said. "And he set the alarm clock and put it in the closet, and he put the vomit and dog stuff on the floor."

" 'He'?" Mr. Harris asked, and looked at Andy.

"And it wasn't Andy," Stacy Ann added.

Mr. Harris folded his hands, leaned back in his chair, and looked at Andy again.

Andy waited for him to say something, but Mr. Harris remained quiet. Andy was uncomfortable being stared at.

Andy looked away, at the large oval table surrounded with chairs in the middle of the room, at the bookcases, and at the many pictures and certificates on the wall. Then he looked at Mr. Harris again.

Mr. Harris was still looking at Andy.

"I didn't do it," Andy said.

The principal didn't respond.

"You can keep looking at me," Andy told the principal, "but I still didn't do it!"

Mr. Harris said, "The most difficult job in any school is being a substitute teacher. You must co-operate with Ms. Salmon."

The telephone on Mr. Harris's desk rang. He picked up the receiver, listened, and said, "I'll be right there," then he put the receiver down.

"Sit, both of you," he told Andy and Stacy Ann as he walked to the door, "and wait for me."

Andy and Stacy Ann waited for Mr. Harris to leave the office. Then they each pulled out a chair and sat at the large oval table in the middle of the room.

"I've been here before," Stacy Ann informed Andy. "I was here when Mrs. Johnson was the principal. She gave me an award for winning the second-grade spelling bee."

"I've also been here before," Andy told Stacy Ann, "for bad stuff."

Andy folded his hands on the table. Then he slowly turned to Stacy Ann and told her, "I'm sorry."

"Why should you be sorry?" Stacy Ann asked. "You didn't do anything wrong. It was Cory."

Andy shook his head and said, "No, it's me. I'm a trouble magnet. I attract trouble and it sticks to me."

There were tears in his eyes as he told his friend, "Yesterday Mr. Harris looked at only one work sheet—mine! And today, I was good. I did the work. I took notes. And look where I am!"

Stacy Ann patted his hand. "This isn't trouble," she told Andy. "I never get into trouble. This is just a misunderstanding. You'll see. Cory will tell Mr. Harris that he did all those stupid tricks. By the end of the day, Mr. Harris and Ms. Salmon will let us back in class."

Andy and Stacy Ann sat quietly for a while.

Andy looked up and counted the ceiling tiles. Then he counted the pictures and certificates on the walls, and the books on the top shelf of the bookcase.

This is torture, Andy thought. *I'm going to die here of boredom.*

RRRR!

The bell rang. It was time for lunch.

Andy and Stacy Ann got up and walked to the door.

"Where are you going?" Mrs. Clark asked them.

"It's time for lunch," Andy told her.

"I'm sorry," she said. "Mr. Harris told me you were to wait until he got back. I'll have someone from your class bring your lunches here."

Andy looked into the hall at all the children walking to the lunchroom.

"Go on," Mrs. Clark said. "Go back in there and sit down."

Andy and Stacy Ann went back into the principal's office. Andy thought about what had happened. Then he turned to Stacy Ann and asked, "Do you know what this taught me?"

Stacy Ann shook her head.

"Not to sharpen my pencil in class," Andy said. "That's why I got into trouble, because I wanted my work to be neat."

"No," Stacy Ann said. "We both got in trouble because Cory wouldn't take the blame for what he did. But I'm just waiting. Either he'll tell Mr. Harris this is all his fault or I will."

Andy looked up at the ceiling again and counted tiles. *I'm a prisoner,* he thought, *a prisoner in the principal's office for something I didn't do.*

Andy put his hand on his stomach. *I'm worse than a prisoner,* he thought. *Prisoners get meals: mashed potatoes or creamed spinach or bread and water! Something!*

"I'm hungry," Andy said to Stacy Ann.

"Me, too," she replied.

Andy looked at the ceiling again and closed his eyes. He thought about all the prisoner movies he had seen, of prisoners kept alone in tiny, dark locked cells, with spiders crawling over them until they confessed their crimes. He thought of prisoners tortured with bright lights.

"That's us," Andy said, and opened his eyes. "We're prisoners in the principal's office. We'll be tortured until we confess."

Andy thought for a moment and then told Stacy Ann, "Mr. Harris is planning to torture us, to starve us until we confess."

Stacy Ann said, "I don't think so."

"Well, I do," Andy said. "You'll see. At the end of the day, we'll be starving and Mr. Harris will dangle cream-cheese sandwiches in front of us. He'll have us confess to all the bad stuff that's ever happened in Ms. Salmon's and Ms. Roman's class."

"Maybe even in the whole school," Stacy Ann said, and smiled.

"Yeah," Andy said. "And after we confess to all that, he'll let us eat the sandwiches. And then the real torture will begin. He'll dangle a container of milk in front of us!"

"Stop it! Stop it!" Stacy Ann said. "You're the one torturing me. You're making me thirsty."

But Andy didn't stop.

"We'll have cream cheese stuck to the roofs of our mouths," he said, "and nothing to drink." Andy lifted his hands high over his head, then bent his fingers to resemble a witch's gnarled hands. "And then," he said in a sinister voice, "he'll dangle a container of ice-cold milk in front of us and holler, '*Confess!*

" 'It was you who made the earthquake in South America!

" 'It was you who caused the floods in Texas!

" 'It was you who stopped up the toilet in the girls' bathroom!

" 'CONFESS!' "

"Yes! Yes!" Stacy Ann shouted. "It was me! It was me!"

Chapter 8
Adults Don't Apologize

Stacy Ann, I can't believe it," Bruce said. "I thought it was Andy."

Bruce was standing by the door to the office. Tamika and Cory were with him.

"We were just playing now," Stacy Ann said. "I didn't do any of those silly jokes in class."

"And I didn't, either," Andy said.

Bruce and Tamika walked into Mr. Harris's office. They put Andy's and Stacy Ann's lunch bags on the table.

Andy and Stacy Ann thanked them.

"You're lucky you were here and not in class," Bruce said. "Ms. Salmon read poetry to us. Her poems don't rhyme like mine do. I didn't understand any of it."

"She's really boring," Tamika said.

"Well," Andy told them, "sitting here with nothing to do is boring, too."

Andy held his lunch bag upside down. A wrapped cream-cheese sandwich, an apple, and a pack of three chocolate-chip cookies fell onto the table.

Bruce said, "We had money for only one milk, and we gave the milk to Cobalt."

Andy held his hands to his throat and said dramatically, "A cream-cheese sandwich and no milk! That's part of the plan. We're being tortured!"

"We'll survive," Stacy Ann said calmly as she took a napkin from her lunch bag and spread it open on the table. She put her sandwich, carrot sticks, and granola bar on the napkin.

Cory was still standing in the doorway. "I'll buy you some milk," he said. "I have money."

"And," Stacy Ann told him, "you should do something else for us."

Then Stacy Ann turned to Bruce and Tamika. "We have to talk to Cory," she told them, *"privately."*

Bruce and Tamika left the office.

As soon as they were gone, Cory said, "I know this is all my fault and I know you're probably angry with me, but do you know how much trouble I'll be in if Mr. Harris finds out I did all that stuff?"

"Do I know? Do I know?" Andy asked. Then he shouted, "Of course I know how much trouble you'd be in, BECAUSE I'M IN IT!"

"No," Stacy Ann corrected Andy, "because *we're* in it."

Cory looked at Andy's lunch and said, "Those cookies look good."

"Don't change the subject," Andy told him.

"Either you tell Mr. Harris and Ms. Salmon that you caused all that trouble," Stacy Ann warned Cory, "or I will."

RRRR!

The bell rang.

Lunchtime was over.

"You'll have to go to class now," Mrs. Clark told Cory. She was standing in the doorway.

"But he has to talk to Mr. Harris," Stacy Ann told Mrs. Clark.

"There was a kindergarten emergency," Mrs. Clark said. "You'll have to talk to Mr. Harris later. Right now you have to go back to class," Mrs. Clark told Cory.

"And the two of you," she said to Andy and Stacy Ann, "have to stay here."

"I'm sorry," Cory told Andy and Stacy Ann, and quickly left the office.

Mrs. Clark returned to her desk.

Andy shrugged.

"Let's eat," he said.

Andy and Stacy Ann sat at the table and ate. First Andy ate his chocolate-chip cookies. Then, between each bite of his cream-cheese sandwich, he bit into his apple.

When they were done eating, Andy threw all the wrappers into the trash can beneath Mr. Harris's desk. Stacy Ann brushed cookie, granola bar, and sandwich crumbs off the table and into her napkin and threw it away.

"Let's play geography," Stacy Ann suggested when she returned to the table.

"No," Andy said. "Not that! All that boring talk of rivers and borders ruined geography for me forever. I may never be able to look at a map again without thinking of boring, fishy Ms. Salmon! Let's play the kindergarten-emergency game instead."

· "The what?"

Andy explained, "We make up kindergarten emergencies that might get Mr. Harris to run out and leave us here."

"I know," Stacy Ann said, "a boy wet his pants and had to be taken home."

"No," Andy said, "use your imagination."

He thought for a moment.

"A spaceship slid down the slide," Andy said, "and landed in the sandbox."

"Aliens got out," Stacy Ann added, "and were playing with the kindergarten blocks." She laughed. "And the aliens won't share the blocks with the children."

Andy closed his eyes and tried to imagine Mr. Harris and the kindergarten teacher trying to convince aliens to share.

"Wake up," someone said.

Andy opened his eyes. It was Mr. Harris. He was standing by the door. Cory was with him.

"I just spoke with Ms. Salmon," Mr. Harris said as he walked with Cory to his desk, "and the two of you can return to class now."

"Great," Stacy Ann said. She walked toward the door.

Andy stood by the table and waited.

"Let's go," Stacy Ann whispered to Andy.

"Go on," Mr. Harris told Andy. "I said you could return to class."

Andy got up and walked slowly to the door. He looked at Mr. Harris and waited.

"Let's go," Stacy Ann whispered again.

Andy turned and started with Stacy Ann back to class.

"Why did you want to stay there?" Stacy Ann asked.

Andy told Stacy Ann, "Mr. Harris shouldn't have just said we could go back to class. He should have apologized to us."

"Maybe," Stacy Ann said, "but I'm just glad we're out of there."

"Ms. Salmon should apologize, too," Andy said. "Both of them accused us of doing things that we didn't do."

"Adults don't apologize," Stacy Ann said.

"Then I can't wait to be an adult," Andy declared. "I won't have to do schoolwork or homework, or apologize."

Andy and Stacy Ann entered their classroom.

Ms. Salmon was standing in the front of the room. She gave Andy and Stacy Ann work sheets and told them, "I don't want any more trouble from either of you. Just sit down and do your work."

"More trouble!" Andy thought. *I haven't given you any trouble!*

He sat in his seat. He put the work sheet on his desk, took out a pencil, and thought, *Stacy Ann is right—adults don't apologize.*

Chapter 9
No Python, No Cobra

There were twenty division problems on the work sheet. This time Andy didn't pick answers at random. He slowly worked the problems out.

Ms. Salmon stood by Andy's and Stacy Ann's desks for a while. She glared down and watched them work and then said, "I see the two of you have learned your lessons."

"WHAT?!" Andy called out.

"That's right," Stacy Ann said quickly. "We're doing our work now."

When Ms. Salmon walked to the front of the room, Stacy Ann turned and whispered to Andy, "She's an adult."

"Yeah," Andy said, "she won't apologize and she still blames us for something we didn't do."

Andy was happy when the bell rang and the school day was over.

Ms. Salmon stood by the door and said, "Goodbye" and "Have a nice day" to most of the students as they walked past her on their way out of the room. But when Andy and Stacy Ann walked past, she told them, "I hope there's no foolishness tomorrow."

Andy was about to respond, when Stacy Ann pulled at his sleeve and said, "Let's go. You don't want to miss your bus."

"Come on," Tamika said. She and Bruce were right behind them. "Mr. Cole can't wait."

"Yeah," Bruce said, "and those cats might not stop the bus today."

Tamika and Bruce pushed Andy out of the room.

"She makes me so mad," Andy said on their way to the bus. When they passed Mr. Harris, Andy added, "And he does, too."

Andy, Tamika, and Bruce sat again on the long seat in the back of the bus.

"Guess what?" Bruce asked Andy.

Andy didn't respond.

"I know," Bruce said, "I know. You don't want to guess, so I'll tell you. I've been studying acting."

Bruce stood.

He raised his right hand and said, " 'To be.' "

He raised his left hand and said, " 'Or not to be.' "

Then Bruce hit his chest with both hands and added, " 'That is the question.' "

He sat down and asked, "How was that?"

"What were you doing?" Andy asked. "I think *that* is the question. And what's all this about bees? They sting, you know."

"I was acting," Bruce explained. "That was from *Hamlet*. It's a real famous play."

Bruce was still talking about acting when the bus came to his stop. Mr. Cole had to remind him again to get off.

Andy, Tamika, Rachel, and the Belmont girls got off at the next stop.

"You know what we should do," Tamika said when they got in the house. "We should make a big get-well card for Ms. Roman, like we did in kindergarten and first grade when someone was absent. Then tomorrow we should get everyone in the class to sign it."

"Why should I help make her a card?" Andy asked. "She's the one who made me do all those extra math problems."

Andy thought for a moment. *Ms. Roman made me do extra math problems for something I did wrong. Ms. Salmon got me in trouble with Mr. Harris for things I didn't do. And Ms. Salmon is so boring.*

"You know what?" Andy said to Tamika. "I'd rather have Ms. Roman as my teacher than Ms. Salmon. But I think we're too old to make one big card. I think each of us should make his own card. Let's call Bruce and Stacy Ann, and they can call the others."

Andy and Tamika made the calls. Then they went to the basement and turned on the computer.

"You can make yours first," Andy told Tamika. "I have to think about mine."

Tamika's card had a picture of flowers on the front. Inside she wrote, *Dear Ms. Roman. I hope*

you get well soon. From your student, Tamika Anderson.

Andy made a rebus card.

He signed the card:

When Mr. and Mrs. Russell came home, Andy and Tamika ran upstairs and showed them the cards.

"That's nice," Mrs. Russell said. "One of the teachers in the high school is a good friend of Ms. Roman's. I'll ask her where we should send the cards."

"Hi, Mom. Hi, Dad," Rachel said as she came downstairs.

Mr. Russell took an envelope from his pocket and said, "I have the pictures. Let's look at them."

"And I'll make dinner," Mrs. Russell said. She took a box from the pantry and added, "No surprises tonight. I'm making macaroni and cheese."

Andy, Tamika, Rachel, and Mr. Russell sat on the living-room couch. Mr. Russell opened the envelope and took out the photographs.

"These are from Grandma's surprise birthday party," he said as he looked at the first few photographs. "That was almost four months ago."

"Look at Mom," Rachel said, "with that silly party hat."

Mrs. Russell came in from the kitchen. She was wearing oven mitts and an apron. "Let me see," she said.

"And let me see the Slither pictures," Andy said. "They were the last ones on the roll."

Mr. Russell gave Andy the pictures from the bottom of the stack.

"Here they are," Andy said. He showed them to Tamika. "Does Slither look like a giant python?"

Tamika sadly shook her head and told Andy,

"No, Slither looks like a skinny garter snake with some toy cars."

Andy looked at the photographs again.

"You know what?" Andy asked, more to himself than to Tamika. "I think for my movie, what I need is a real python."

Mrs. Russell said firmly, "And you're not getting one!"

"A cobra?" Andy asked.

"No," his mother answered. "You're not getting a cobra, either. What you're getting is dinner. Just as soon as I finish making it."

But Mrs. Russell didn't rush back to the kitchen. She continued to look at the photographs.

Tamika was looking at them, too.

"Come on," Andy said to her. "Let's go downstairs and show these pictures to Slither."

Tamika didn't seem to hear him. She was looking intently at a photograph of Andy's family. There were tears in her eyes.

"What's wrong?" Andy asked.

Tamika looked at Andy, but she didn't answer him. She looked at Mr. and Mrs. Russell, and Rachel, and then dropped the photograph and ran from the room.

"What happened?" Mrs. Russell asked.

Andy shrugged. He didn't know.

"Andy said something stupid," Rachel declared. "That's what happened."

"I only said, 'Let's show these pictures to Slither,' and I asked, 'What's wrong?' It wasn't anything I said. It's probably Rachel's fault. She's always complaining about sharing her room with Tamika."

Mrs. Russell gave the photographs she was holding to Mr. Russell. She gave him the oven mitts and apron, too.

"Please," she told him, "finish making dinner. We're going up to Tamika."

Tamika was on her bed, in the room she shared with Rachel. She was crying. The door was open. Mrs. Russell reached in and knocked on it.

Tamika looked up. She wiped her eyes with the back of her hand.

"May we come in?" Mrs. Russell asked.

Tamika nodded.

Mrs. Russell sat on the bed, next to Tamika. Andy and Rachel stood nearby.

"Please," Mrs. Russell quietly said, "tell me what's wrong."

Tamika wiped her eyes again. "I looked at the

pictures of the party," she said. "You were all smiling. And I looked at all of you. Your family is together. But mine isn't. My parents are in wheelchairs. My dad can hardly talk." Tamika turned away.

Mrs. Russell reached out and took her hand. "Your parents are getting better," Mrs. Russell told her. "Soon you'll all be together, too."

"And you're part of our family," Andy said.

"I know sometimes I yell at you, but I love you. We all do," Rachel said.

Tamika turned. There were tears in her eyes and on her cheeks.

"I know," she said. "You're my friends, my very good friends, but you're not my family." She wiped away the tears. "I'm here, and the rest of my family is in the rehabilitation center."

Mrs. Russell took Tamika's hand again and said, "It's already Thursday. Sunday is just a few more days and you'll see your parents. I know how much you look forward to those visits." She thought for a moment and then added, "Seeing you always makes them feel better. It may even help them *get* better."

Everyone was quiet for a while. Mrs. Russell

still held Tamika's hand. And Andy stood there, awkwardly, with his head down. He was uncomfortable being with Tamika when she was so upset, but he knew it would be wrong for him to leave.

After what seemed to Andy to be a long while, Mrs. Russell patted Tamika's hand and said, "Come. Let's go downstairs and see what Dad did with the noodles and cheese."

Andy was the first one out of Rachel and Tamika's room, and the first one in the kitchen.

The lights were off. The table was set, and on each plate was a cupcake wrapper filled with macaroni and cheese. In the center of each cup was a lit birthday candle.

Andy sat in his seat and waited.

"What's this?" Mrs. Russell asked when she came into the kitchen.

Mr. Russell shrugged and said, "I was just having fun."

Mrs. Russell and Rachel blew out their candles.

"Hey," Rachel complained as she started to eat, "there's wax in my noodles!"

Andy looked down. His candle was still burning. He watched wax drip onto his noodles. Then he looked across the table at Tamika. Her eyes were closed and her lips were moving. *She's making a wish,* Andy thought.

Tamika opened her eyes and blew out her candle.

Andy closed his eyes. *I have a wish, too,* Andy thought. *It's that Tamika's wish comes true.* Andy squeezed his eyes shut. *And soon,* Andy added, *real soon.*

Andy opened his eyes. He blew out his candle, took a forkful of macaroni, cheese, and wax, and started to eat.

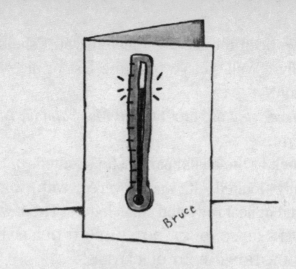

Chapter 10
Adults Do Apologize

Sit in your seats!" Ms. Salmon said the next morning when Andy, Tamika, and Bruce entered the classroom. "Sit!" she said again when other children came in.

Andy and the others quickly sat in their seats and waited.

Ms. Salmon's arms were folded. She glared down at Andy and his classmates as she paced the room.

"I've been too nice, too nice to you," she said angrily. "Well, you've seen the last of nice Ms. Salmon!"

I never saw the first *of* nice *Ms. Salmon,* Andy thought.

"Look at the chalkboard!" she shouted.

Andy looked. It was covered with words, printed in neat rows and small letters. There were 12 RULES OF CONDUCT, NOTES ABOUT OUR RIVERS, and QUESTIONS ABOUT OUR RIVERS.

"Copy the rules on a clean sheet of paper," Ms. Salmon instructed as she continued to pace the room. "And copy the geography notes, too."

Ms. Salmon stopped by Andy's desk. Her arms were folded. "Read rule seven," she told him. "I wrote it especially for you."

Andy read rule seven.

"Stand," she told him, "and read it aloud."

Andy stood by his desk and read rule seven: " 'I must act with great respect for my teacher at all times.' "

"That means no silly faces!" Ms. Salmon told Andy. "Now sit, and when you get to rule seven, copy it fifty times."

While Andy copied what was written on the

chalkboard, he looked across the aisle to Cory Davis's seat. It was empty.

I should have stayed home, too, Andy thought. *I'm stuck here, and Cory is probably watching television now, or playing games.*

Andy wrote until the point on his pencil was gone. But he refused to sharpen it. With his thumbnail, he peeled off some of the wood near his pencil point and kept writing.

By the time the bell rang for lunch, Andy's hand hurt.

Some children closed their books and stood. They were about to go to the closet and get their lunch bags.

"Stop!" Ms. Salmon shouted. "That sound you heard was not for you. It was a signal to me. Now, if *I'm* ready, I may dismiss you."

She looked across the room.

"But I'm *not* ready," she declared. "Now, go on with your work."

"I'm hungry," one child said.

"Ms. Roman never makes us wait to eat," someone else said.

But the children sat again. They opened their books and continued their work.

A few minutes later, Ms. Salmon announced, "*Now* I'm ready. You may go to lunch."

Andy closed his book, got his lunch, and hurried out of the room.

"I hate her," Andy told Tamika, Bruce, and Stacy Ann in the lunchroom.

"And she hates you," Tamika told Andy.

Stacy Ann said, "I think she hates all of us."

Several children came to their table and said they had made cards for Ms. Roman. They told Andy and Tamika they would give them the cards after school. Then they sat down at Andy's table and the one next to it.

"Oh," Bruce told them all, "wait till you see my card. On the front, I drew a thermometer with the red line really long because Ms. Roman probably has a fever. And I wrote a poem inside."

Bruce stood, put his arms straight at his sides, and recited his poem in a singsong:

> *"Dear Ms. Roman,*
> *here's my poem, and*
> *since you're sick,*
> *get well quick."*

Bruce smiled and bowed slightly.

"That was very nice," Nicole Adams said. "I'm sure Ms. Roman will really like it."

"Yes," Tamika agreed.

"It's creative," Bruce told them. "Dad said, smart people understand things, but it's creative people like me who change the world."

And it's people like me who hate poetry, Andy thought, *and change the* subject.

"Cory was smart to stay home," Andy said. "I wish I was home, too."

"Cory's not home. He's here," Brian Baker said. "I came to school with him. Mr. Harris stopped him in the hall and said, 'Young man, come with me.'"

"'Young man,'" Andy said, imitating Mr. Harris's deep voice, "'come with me.'"

Suddenly Andy had a frightening thought. He slowly turned and looked behind him.

Children were sitting at tables and eating. Some were at the counter, buying pretzels, fruit, and milk. Mr. Harris was in the lunchroom, too, but he was by the doors to the playground, too far away to have heard Andy.

I was almost in trouble again, Andy thought.

Andy went to the counter and bought two containers of milk, one for him and one for Cobalt, the kitten on the school playground. Andy ate his cream-cheese sandwich, apple, and chocolate-chip cookies. He opened one container of milk and drank from it.

Brian Baker said, "I should have brought my laughing box to school. Wouldn't it be great if each time Ms. Salmon turned around, I opened the box and it started laughing?"

"Ms. Salmon would get so angry," Bruce said.

Tamika told Brian, "She'd take you right to Mr. Harris's office."

Andy shook his head and said sadly, "No, she'd take me and maybe she'd take Stacy Ann, too."

Andy gathered the wrappers from his sandwich and cookies, his apple core, and empty milk container and put them in his empty lunch bag. He picked up his extra container of milk.

"She's a substitute," Brian said. "We have to do *something* this afternoon."

"Well," Andy said, "right now I'm going outside.

And when I go back to class, I'm going to try to stay out of trouble."

Andy threw his lunch bag away. Then he, Tamika, Bruce, and Stacy Ann went outside.

They walked to the corner of the playground near the trash cans. Andy opened the second container of milk all the way and put it on the ground. A dark gray kitten with a white face, chest, and feet peeked out from between the trash cans and ran to the milk. She lapped it up and pushed over the container with her paws so she could get the last remaining drops.

Stacy Ann had brought a can of cat food. She opened the can, held it out, and called, "Here, Cobalt."

The kitten ran to her. Stacy Ann put the can on the ground.

As they watched Cobalt eat, Andy said, "Ms. Salmon keeps looking at me in class. She makes me feel like a criminal."

"Isn't she cute?" Stacy Ann asked.

" 'Cute'!" Andy shouted. "You call her cute?"

Cobalt stopped eating and looked at Andy. Tamika, Bruce, and Stacy Ann looked at him, too.

Andy said, "Ms. Salmon makes my skin crawl! My hair curl! My eyes bulge! My ears pop! And you call her *cute!*"

"I was talking about Cobalt," Stacy Ann explained as she petted the kitten.

Andy looked at his friends and said, "Oh."

RRRR!

The bell rang. Lunchtime was over, and Andy hurried back to class.

Open your notebook to your science section and await instruction was written on the chalkboard.

Andy opened his notebook to a blank page and waited with his hands folded for Ms. Salmon to begin the lesson.

Ms. Salmon stood in front of the room. There was an open book on her desk. When everyone was seated she said, "This afternoon I will teach you about the force of gravity."

Ms. Salmon paced slowly as she spoke. She looked at the children's notebooks to be sure they were ready to take notes.

"If you throw a ball up, it always comes down," she said. "It's pulled down to earth. That pull is the force of gravity."

Ms. Salmon walked to the front of the room. She looked in the open book on her desk and then said, "Isaac Newton discovered the pull of gravity in 1665."

She turned and as she wrote *Isaac Newton* on the chalkboard, someone made cat sounds.

Meow! Meow!

Ms. Salmon turned quickly. The meowing stopped. The children were all busy writing in their notebooks.

Ms. Salmon slowly turned to the chalkboard again. Following *Isaac Newton,* she wrote, *was born in England in 1642.*

Ruff! Ruff!

Grrr!

Tweet! Tweet!

Roar!

Oink! Oink!

Ms. Salmon turned. She looked directly at Andy and shouted, "That was not funny!"

Andy put his pencil down.

"You have no respect, do you?" Ms. Salmon asked as she walked toward him.

Andy didn't answer her. He felt defeated. *No*

matter what I do, he thought, *I get in trouble.* Tears were forming in his eyes, but he refused to cry.

Ms. Salmon stood next to Andy's desk. She pointed around the room and said, "These children want to learn and you won't let them! You think animal noises are more important than education!"

"I don't think that," Andy protested.

"It's not easy being a substitute teacher," Ms. Salmon said softly.

"I know it's not easy," Andy said. "But I'm only one person. I couldn't have made all those sounds."

Ms. Salmon thought about that.

Andy thought, *Finally she believes me.*

"And yesterday," Andy told Ms. Salmon, "I didn't make faces behind your back. I was just sharpening my pencil. Everyone was laughing because of that sign on your pants."

"Oh," Ms. Salmon said.

Ms. Salmon turned and slowly returned to her desk. She pulled out her chair and sat down. She looked at Andy and asked, "Are you telling me you did nothing wrong?"

"I didn't make faces or animal noises," he said, "but I did get lots of math problems wrong."

Ms. Salmon was quiet for a moment. Then she said slowly, "This is my first teaching job. I'm sure I did lots of things wrong, too."

Everyone was quiet for a while. Then Brian Baker stood and said, "I did. I went *meow* and *ruff, ruff.*"

Nicole Adams stood, too. "You should yell at me, not Andy," she said. "I growled."

"I roared," Darryl Stein said. He stood, too.

"And I made the bird sounds," Jason Travers told Ms. Salmon, and stood by his seat.

Jane Polk stood and said, "I was the one who oinked."

Ms. Salmon looked at Andy. Then one by one, she looked at each of the five children who were standing. Andy was sure Ms. Salmon would scream at them and send them to Mr. Harris's office.

She didn't.

"You were wrong for making animal noises in class," Ms. Salmon said to Brian, Nicole, Darryl, Jason, and Jane, "and I was wrong for blaming Andy."

Ms. Salmon got up and walked to Andy's desk. "I'm sorry," she said to Andy.

She thought for a moment and then told Andy and Stacy Ann, "And I'm sorry I sent the two of you to Mr. Harris's office. I was wrong to do that, too."

Brian raised his hand and said, "I'm sorry I disturbed your lesson." He spoke in almost a whisper.

Ms. Salmon nodded and Brian sat down.

Nicole, Darryl, Jason, and Jane said they were sorry, too, and sat down.

Ms. Salmon walked to the front of the room. She smiled and said, "Why don't we all forget my first few days here. It's Friday afternoon. Let's finish the school week with a game. We'll make up a chain story. We'll take turns adding sentences to a story. Who wants to start?"

Nicole Adams raised her hand. When Ms. Salmon acknowledged her, Nicole stood and said, "I am a chain and this is my story."

Tamika added, "It's a twisted, tangled, very long story."

Andy smiled. Then he looked at Ms. Salmon and thought, *Stacy Ann was wrong. Adults do apologize.*

Chapter 11
Visiting Ms. Roman

When the bell rang and the school day ended, many of the children in the class gave Andy cards for Ms. Roman. Andy put them in his backpack and hurried to the bus.

"What happened in class today was like what happens sometimes when we play baseball," Bruce said to Andy and Tamika on their way home.

"What?" Andy and Tamika asked.

"You know," Bruce explained, "sometimes one

of us throws the ball and thinks it's a strike. The other person thinks it's a ball, so we have a 'do-over.' That's what we had in class."

"Hey, you're right," Andy said. "She had a bad time with us. Stacy Ann and I had a bad time with her, so we had a 'do-over.' "

Tamika was in the seat by the window. She looked out. "I wish we could all do over bad times," she said softly, "especially my parents."

Yeah, Andy thought. *I wish they could do over the time of the car accident.*

When they got home, Andy and Tamika fed Sylvia and the gerbils.

As Andy changed the water in Slither's bowl, he told the snake, "I'm sorry, but you failed your screen test. You won't be a movie star."

Slither didn't respond.

"Maybe you could become an air conditioner repairman or a scientist."

Slither stuck his forked tongue into the water and had a drink. Then he turned and stuck his tongue out at Andy.

"Well, you think it over," Andy told Slither.

Andy looked in the next tank and watched the gerbils run through their tunnels.

Tamika said, "I'll be right back."

She ran up the stairs. When she came back, she was holding a small piece of paper.

"I have Cory's telephone number," she told Andy. "I'm going to call him and find out what happened with Mr. Harris."

Tamika dialed the telephone and waited.

"Hello, Cory? . . . This is Tamika . . . what happened to you today?"

Tamika waited and listened for a long time. Then she said, "That's good. I'll see you on Monday."

Tamika put the telephone down and told Andy, "At the end of the day, Ms. Salmon met Cory in Mr. Harris's office. Cory apologized, and Ms. Salmon said he could come back to class on Monday."

"Hi!" Mrs. Russell called to Andy and Tamika, from the top of the basement stairs. "I have some news about Ms. Roman."

Andy checked that the screens on the gerbils' and Slither's tanks were completely closed. Then he followed Tamika and his mother to the kitchen.

"I spoke to Mrs. Rosen today. She's Ms. Roman's friend," Mrs. Russell said. She was cutting vegetables while she spoke, for the salad for dinner. "Ms. Roman is doing well. We can visit her." Mrs. Russell wiped her eyes with the back of her hand.

"She's in the hospital connected to the rehabilitation center. On Sunday, when you go to see your parents, Tamika," Mrs. Russell said, "we'll visit Ms. Roman."

Mrs. Russell wiped her eyes again and said, "Please get me a tissue."

Tamika took one from the box on the kitchen table and gave it to Mrs. Russell.

"Ms. Roman is really sick, isn't she?" Andy asked. "That's why you're crying."

"No," Mrs. Russell said. "She *is* doing well. Mrs. Rosen said she loves having visitors. It's the onion that's making me cry."

On Sunday morning Andy and Tamika put all the get-well cards for Ms. Roman in a large manila envelope. It was a short drive to the hospital and rehabilitation center.

The Russells bought two bouquets at the gift shop, one for Ms. Roman and one for Tamika's parents. Then they went to the front desk.

"You're both a little young to be visiting a hospital patient," the woman behind the desk told Andy and Tamika.

Mrs. Russell said, "The children will be in the room for only a few minutes. Ms. Roman is their teacher."

Andy held up the manila envelope and said, "The kids in our class made get-well cards. We want to give them to her."

"And I just want to say hello," Tamika said. "Then I'm going to visit my parents. They're in the rehabilitation center."

"OK," the woman replied, and gave Mrs. Russell visitors' passes. "Go ahead."

The Russells and Tamika rode the elevator to the sixth floor. They went to room 613. The door was open. "May we come in?" Mrs. Russell asked.

Ms. Roman called out, "Of course you may."

Andy followed his parents and Tamika into the room. There were two beds. An old woman with short white hair was in the first one. Ms. Roman was in the bed near the window. She was sitting up. There were lots of books and magazines on the small table next to her. "I'm so happy to see you," she said.

"Here," Andy replied, and gave her the envelope.

Ms. Roman took the cards out. "How nice," she said. She put the cards on the small table. "I'll read them later."

"How are you?" Mrs. Russell asked.

"I feel a lot better now," Ms. Roman answered. "I feel stronger."

"That's good," Tamika said.

Ms. Roman introduced the Russells and Tamika to Mrs. Nelson, the woman in the other bed.

"Well," Mrs. Russell said, "I'm glad you're feeling better. Now I'm going to take Tamika next door, to visit her parents in the rehabilitation center." She and Tamika left the room.

Mr. Russell told Ms. Roman, "And I'll get a vase for the flowers." He left the room, too.

Andy was alone with Ms. Roman and Mrs. Nelson. *This room smells like medicine,* he thought.

"This young man is one of my favorite students," Ms. Roman told Mrs. Nelson.

"I am?" Andy asked.

"Of course you are," Ms. Roman told him. "You don't always pay attention, but sometimes that's my fault. I know some of my lessons are boring."

"You're not so boring," Andy said, "but Ms. Salmon is. She's the substitute. She talks on and on about rivers and borders and states, and makes us copy lots of things from the board. This is her first teaching job, so she's not so good at it yet."

Andy looked down at his shoes and at the floor, and said, "We miss you."

Ms. Roman said, "I miss you, too."

Andy looked at Ms. Roman and asked, "What's wrong with you?"

Ms. Roman put her hand on her chest and said, "It's my heart. I have a weak heart."

Andy looked at Ms. Roman and thought of the many times she had helped him in class. He remembered that she never blamed him for something he didn't do, and how gentle she had been with his gerbils when they got loose.

"No," Andy said, and shook his head. "No, you don't. You have a *good* heart."

Ms. Roman smiled.

"And I hope you get all better," Andy told her, "real soon."

Turn the page for a sneak peek at Andy's next adventure....

Now that Andy Russell's school trouble is over, it's time for a great adventure away from home. When Tamika's aunt and uncle invite Andy and Tamika to the big city, Andy can't wait to experience the excitement of city life. But boring ballets and stuffy restaurants aren't exactly the diversions that Andy expected.

As if that wasn't bad enough, someone is throwing hamsters tied to parachutes from an apartment above Aunt Mandy's. It's a job for Detective Andy Russell to find out who that someone is, as he spends an eventful day with Tamika, Aunt Mandy, and a bratty upstairs-neighbor boy named Jason. Read *Parachuting Hamsters and Andy Russell* to find out whether Andy can manage to stay out of hot water far from home!

Join Andy in all of his adventures! If you liked
School Trouble for Andy Russell, you'll enjoy reading
the other books in this exciting series about Andy,
his friends, and his never-ending escapades.